Turtle and Snail

Turtle and Snail

by Zibby Oneal

Pictures by Margot Tomes

A Lippincott I-Like-To-Read Book

J. B. Lippincott Company
Philadelphia and New York

Text copyright © 1979 by Zibby Oneal
Illustrations copyright © 1979 by Margot Tomes
All Rights Reserved
Printed in the United States of America
2 4 6 8 9 7 5 3 1

U.S. Library of Congress Cataloging in Publication Data

Oneal, Zibby.
 Turtle and snail.

 (A Lippincott I-like-to-read book)
 SUMMARY: Five episodes in which a turtle and a snail demonstrate
their fondness for and loyalty to each other.
 [1. Snails—Fiction. 2. Turtles—Fiction. 3. Friendship—Fiction] I.
Tomes, Margot. II. Title.
PZ7.0552Tu   [E]   78-14826   ISBN-0-397-31829-4

TO BOB

Contents

A Friend

Snail sat under a tulip. "I want a friend," Snail said. "I am lonely."

Ant ran by. "Will you be my friend?" Snail said.

"Not now," said Ant. "It is going to rain. I am going to hide in a hole. Come with me."

"I can't," said Snail. "My shell won't fit."

"Sorry," said Ant, and she hurried on.

"Nobody wants a friend in a shell," Snail said. "And I am still lonely."

Next Grasshopper hopped by.

"Maybe this is a friend," Snail said. "Will you be my friend, Grasshopper?"

"Not now," said Grasshopper. "It is going to rain. I have to hop under a leaf to keep my wings dry. Come with me."

"I can't," said Snail. "A shell can't hop."

"Sorry," said Grasshopper, and he
hopped on.

"Nobody wants a friend in a shell," Snail said. "A shell can't hop. A shell won't fit in a hole. And I am still lonely."

Then Baby Robin came jumping by.

"Robin," said Snail, "will you be my friend?"

"Not now," said Robin. "It is going to rain. I have to fly to my nest. Come with me."

"I can't," said Snail. "A shell can't fly."

"Jump out of your shell," Baby Robin said. "I did."

"I can't," said Snail.

"Try," said Robin.

Snail tried.

"You see?" Snail said. "A snail is stuck."

"Sorry," Baby Robin said, and he flew away.

"Nobody wants a friend in a shell," Snail said. "A shell can't fly. A shell can't hop. A shell won't fit in a hole. And I am still lonely."

Just then it began to rain. "It is raining," Snail said. "I have no friend. I have no place to go. All I have is my dumb old shell. If I could, I would kick it."

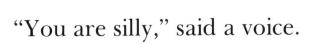

"You are silly," said a voice.

Snail looked up. There was Turtle.

"Put your head in your shell,"
Turtle said. "That is what a shell is
for. A shell keeps off the rain. Robin
has a nest. Ant has a hole. You have a
shell. So do I."

Snail laughed. "I never thought of
that," Snail said. "Now I have a place
to go."

"And now you have a friend," said
Turtle.

"I have a friend in a shell," said Snail.

"I have a friend in a shell," said Turtle.

Then Snail and Turtle sat in the rain together, listening to raindrops falling on their shells.

Mud Pie

It was Turtle's birthday. Snail
wanted to give Turtle a present.
"Turtles like mud," Snail said. "I will
make Turtle a mud pie."

Fly flew by. "What is *that?*" Fly said.

"That is a mud pie for Turtle," said
Snail. "This is Turtle's birthday."

"Turtles don't eat mud," Fly said.
"Turtles eat flies." Then Fly flew
away fast.

"I guess I know what my friend
eats," Snail said. And he kept on
making the mud pie.

Ant came by. "What is *that*?" Ant said.

"That is a mud pie for Turtle," said Snail. "This is Turtle's birthday."

"Turtles don't eat mud," Ant said. "Turtles eat ants." Then Ant crawled away fast.

"I guess I know what my friend eats," Snail said. And he kept on making the mud pie.

Bee buzzed by. "What is *that?*" Bee said.

"That is a mud pie for Turtle,"
said Snail. "This is Turtle's birthday."

"Turtles don't eat mud," Bee said.
"Turtles eat ants and flies. If turtles
try to eat bees, we sting them." Then
Bee laughed and buzzed away.

"Fly is dumb. Ant is dumb. Bee is
dumb," Snail said. "I guess I know
what my friend eats." And he kept on
making the mud pie.

When the mud pie was made, Snail
put it on his back. He carried it to
Turtle's house.

"Turtles don't eat flies.
Turtles don't eat ants.
Turtles don't eat bees.
Turtles eat mud!"

Snail sang on the way.

Turtle was sitting in the sun.

"Happy birthday, Turtle," Snail said.
"I have brought you a present."

"Thank you, Snail," said Turtle. "I
see you have brought me some mud."

"Yes," said Snail. "Fly said you like
flies. Ant said you like ants. Bee said
you might try bees. But I am your
friend. I know you like mud."

"I do," said Turtle. He looked at the mud pie. Then he sat down on it.

"Why are you sitting on your pie?" Snail cried. "Why? Why? Your pie is to eat!"

"Turtles don't eat mud," Turtle said. "They sit in it."

Snail pulled his head into his shell. "Fly and Ant and Bee were right," Snail said. "And I am a dumb friend."

"Turtles *love* to sit in mud," Turtle said. "And this is a good present."

But Snail didn't hear. He was too far inside his shell.

Help

Snail was sad.

"I need a new friend now," Snail said. "I gave Turtle a mud pie. Turtle thinks I am dumb."

Snail looked around. He saw Ant. He saw Baby Robin. He saw Fly. He saw Grasshopper.

"Turtle was a good friend," Snail said. "Turtle had a shell like me."

27

Ant ran down a hole. Baby Robin
flew up to his nest. Fly flew off.
Grasshopper hopped away.

"Maybe I will go see Turtle just one
more time," Snail said.

Snail went to Turtle's house.
Turtle was not there. "Turtle,
Turtle," Snail called. "It is me. Snail."

Nobody answered.

"Maybe Turtle moved away," Snail said. "Now I have no friend at all."

Then Snail heard a small voice. "Help!" the voice said.

"Is that you, Turtle?" said Snail.

"Help!" said the voice.

Snail looked around.

"Here I am!" said the voice.

"Where?" said Snail.

"Here I am in the tall grass. Help!"

Snail found Turtle. Turtle was lying in the tall grass.

"Why are you lying in the tall grass, Turtle? Why are you lying in the tall grass on your back?" Snail said.

"I tipped over," Turtle said.

"Stand up," said Snail, "and we will go have a picnic."

"I can't," said Turtle. "I am stuck."

"I will help," said Snail.

Snail pushed Turtle. Turtle did not turn.

Snail pushed harder. Turtle did not turn.

Snail pushed very hard. Turtle stayed stuck on his back.

"Do not go away," Snail said. "I will help you."

Snail went home fast.

"Ant, help me turn Turtle," Snail said.

"Fly, help me turn Turtle," Snail said.

"I will help," said Ant.

"I will help," said Fly.

"So will I," said Grasshopper.

"So will I," said Baby Robin.

"All together we will turn Turtle," Snail said.

Ant and Fly and Grasshopper and Baby Robin went to Turtle's house. They went with Snail.

"Help!" said Turtle.

"We will help," they said.

Ant pushed. Fly pushed. Grasshopper and Baby Robin pushed. Snail pushed hardest of all.

"I am turning," said Turtle.

They all pushed together.

Turtle turned! Turtle stood on his feet. "Thank you," said Turtle.

"You are a good friend, Snail," Turtle said.

"We are all good friends," said
Snail.

Turtle found some cookies for his
friends.

"Do not tip over again," said Snail.

"I won't," said Turtle.

Lost and Found

Snail and Turtle went on a picnic. The sun was shining. They went to the woods.

Snail brought peanut butter sandwiches. Turtle brought lemonade.

Turtle ate the peanut butter sandwiches. Snail drank the lemonade.

Soon all the peanut butter
sandwiches were gone. Soon all the
lemonade was gone.

"That was a good picnic," Snail said. "Now I am sleepy."

"That was a good picnic," said Turtle. "Now we will go home."

Turtle started out. "Which way is home?" Turtle said. "This way?"

Turtle walked toward a tall tree. "Is this the way home?"

"No," said Snail.

Turtle walked toward the river. "Is this the way home?"

"No," said Snail.

Turtle walked toward the tall grass. "Is this the way home?"

"That is not the way home," Snail said.

"That is not the way and this is not the way and that is not the way," Turtle said. "Snail, we are lost!"

Turtle began to cry.

"I want to go home!" Turtle cried. "I do not want to be lost in the woods! The peanut butter sandwiches are gone! The lemonade is gone! I want to go home!"

"I know the way home," Snail said.

Turtle stopped crying. "You do?" Turtle said.

"Yes, I do," said Snail. "We can follow my trail."

"What is your trail?" said Turtle.

"Snails leave a trail wherever they go," Snail said. "That is what snails do."

"Where is your trail?" said Turtle.

"Behind me."

Turtle looked. He saw Snail's trail.

"My trail comes out of my shell," said Snail. "I walk on it."

"I wish I were a snail," said Turtle. "Then I would never be lost."

"You can use my trail," Snail said. "Because you are my friend."

Turtle and Snail went home. The sun was shining on Snail's trail. They followed it.

Remember?

Turtle was sitting in the sun. Snail was sitting in the shade.

Snail liked shade. Turtle liked sun. They were happy.

"Do you remember when we sat in the rain?" Snail said.

"Yes, I do," said Turtle.

"And do you remember when I made you a mud pie and you sat on it?"

"That was a good present," said Turtle.

"And do you remember when you tipped over in the tall grass?"

"Help!" said Turtle.

"And do you remember when we were lost in the woods and we followed my trail?"

"Yes, I do," said Turtle.

"I remember, too," said Snail.

"Do you remember when we laughed all day?" Turtle said.

"No, I don't," said Snail.

"That is because we have not done it yet," Turtle said. "We will do it now. Then you will remember."

"All right," said Snail.

So they did.

About the Author

Zibby Oneal teaches a course in writing at the University of Michigan. *Turtle and Snail* is her third book. Ms. Oneal lives in Ann Arbor, Michigan, with her husband.

About the Artist

Margot Tomes's distinctive illustrations have appeared in over two dozen children's books. Ms. Tomes lives in New York City.